For Jesse—the world
—R.S.

To Libby, colorful friend and loving mama, for all you give
—S.S.G.

Text copyright © 2006 by Roni Schotter
Cover and interior illustrations copyright © 2006 by S. Saelig Gallagher

Dragonfly Books with the colophon is a registered trademark of Random House, Inc.

Visit us on the Web!
randomhouse.com/kids

Educators and librarians, for a variety of teaching tools, visit us at
RHTeachersLibrarians.com

The Library of Congress has cataloged the hardcover edition of this work as follows:
Schotter, Roni.
Mama, I'll give you the World / Roni Schotter ; illustrated by Susan Saelig Gallagher. — 1st ed.
p. cm.
Summary: At Walter's World of Beauty, Luisa's secret plans are underway
to create a very special birthday celebration for her hard-working, single mother who is employed there as a stylist.
ISBN 978-0-375-83612-1 (trade) — ISBN 978-0-375-93612-8 (lib. bdg.) — ISBN 978-0-449-81143-6 (ebook)
[1. Birthdays—Fiction. 2. Single-parent families—Fiction. 3. Beauty shops—Fiction.]
I. Gallagher, Susan, ill. II. Title.
PZ7.S3765Mam 2006b
[Fic]—dc22
2005021987

ISBN 978-0-449-81142-9 (pbk.)

MANUFACTURED IN CHINA
10 9 8 7 6 5 4 3 2 1
First Dragonfly Books Edition

Mama, I'll Give You the World

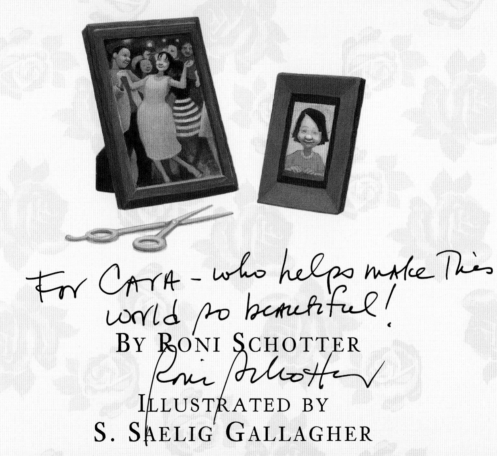

For CARA — who helps make This
world so beautiful!

BY RONI SCHOTTER

Roni Schotter

ILLUSTRATED BY
S. SAELIG GALLAGHER

Dragonfly Books ⸺✦ New York

When Papa was around, Mama loved to dance, but Mama doesn't dance anymore. She works hard every day at Walter's World of Beauty, cutting, coloring, and curling.

After school each afternoon, Luisa's bus drops
her at the door to the World. Everyone greets her—
Walter, Rupa, Georges, but especially Mama.

Mama smiles and makes a place for Luisa—on a
cushion, under the palm tree. "First things first,"
Mama always says, so there by Walter's Bottles
of Beauty, with names that whisper promises—
Raspberry Radiance, Evening Glamour Glow,
Sunday Night Soother—Luisa does her schoolwork.

While Mama, like a magician, turns Mrs. Koo's dark hair the color of sunset, Walter, Georges, and Rupa cut and comb.

Luisa does a math problem. Then she writes a story for English about a girl with a magic brush that brushes people's cares away.

When she finishes her homework, Luisa takes out her scissors, her glue, and her paper and does what Mama does—cuts and colors and curls—portraits of the customers. "Everyone in the world is a flower," her mother always tells her. "Together, they make a bouquet." So Luisa cuts slowly, noticing how different each flower is, and how each one comes in a special size and shape.

In between customers, Mama rests in her chair and lets Luisa brush her long, thick curls. Luisa brushes hard, pretending she is the girl in her story, carefully watching her mother's face to see if she can make her smile. Mama hardly ever smiles, but when she does, she is the prettiest flower in the World.

Luisa loves to look at the pictures at her mother's station. One is of Luisa; the other is of Mama long ago—happy and *dancing*—in a large room that looks like a palace, crowded with people and full of lights. Mama says the name of the palace is Roseland, but Luisa doesn't believe her. She thinks her mother has made up the name because she loves flowers.

"Can we go there?"
Luisa asks. She imagines
the two of them holding
hands and dancing at the
palace Mama calls Roseland. . . .

But Mama shakes her head, no.
She holds the picture in her hands, and
her eyes look at something far away and once
upon a time—something Luisa can only guess at.

Under the dryers, the ladies loudly whisper their secrets, but Luisa has a secret of her own. Tomorrow is Mama's birthday, and tonight Luisa is going to give her the present she's been planning for such a long time.

For the past few weeks, whenever Mama isn't looking, Luisa
has whispered her secret in the ear of each of Mama's favorite customers—

—when she sweeps up snippets of hair for
handsome Mr. Anselmo, who always tells Mama,
"Just a little off here and a little off there,
please leave it as long as you dare,
for you see, don't you know?
You can see it is so, that I
haven't a lot left
to spare."

—when she helps Mrs. Malloy, bent
over and sad as she inches into
the World on her walker, but
smiling and standing nearly straight
an hour later, when,
feeling beautiful
again, she leaves.

—when she helps Mama
brush and braid Hazel Mae
Dixon's go-everywhere
hair till it looks like
neat, shiny rows
of licorice.

—when she sprays fussy Mrs. Fogelman's
hair that refuses to stand up and obey
until Mama teases it with a comb so
it can't *help* standing up—fluffy
and high as a great, gray cloud,
just the way Mrs. Fogelman likes it!

—and when she removes the giant
pink and purple rollers that turn
Mrs. Rodriguez's dark
tangles into an ocean
of gentle waves.

At six o'clock it's time at last to go home. Luisa exchanges secret winks with Walter, Georges, and Rupa. Then she and Mama hang up their smocks and empty their pockets, heavy with tip money.

It all goes into a special envelope. "First things first," Mama says. She
is saving for Luisa—for college. Mama wants Luisa to learn *everything*.

Outside, the world stretches before them—dark, mysterious, and twinkling with store- and street- and starlight. Luisa and Mama stand together looking at it, feeling oh, so small. Mama's hair sparkles in the light. So do her eyes.

"The world is big. So much more for you to know. So much more for you to see. One day, if I can," Mama says, patting the envelope deep in her coat pocket, "I will give the world to you."

No, thinks Luisa. Tonight, if I can, I will give the world to *you* . . . for your birthday!

At home that evening Luisa asks Mama
to try on her prettiest dress—the one
with the roses and violets and vines
that encircle Mama's waist the way
Luisa's arms do when they hug.
"Please, Mama?" Luisa begs.

"Not now," Mama says. "I'm tired."

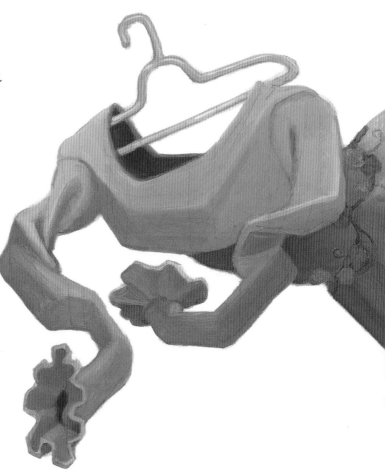

"Pretty please?" Luisa asks,
opening her eyes as wide
as Walter's windows
and looking at Mama
in a way she knows
Mama can't refuse.

"Allll right," Mama says, and puts on her dress. While she does, Luisa pretends to be searching for something. "Mama!" she calls out. "We have to go back to the World! I forgot my book." Luisa hurries and hands Mama her coat.

Mama pushes the coat away. "No," she says. "It can wait until tomorrow."

Luisa is worried. "But Mama," she pleads. "It's for my *book report*. Don't you always tell me 'first things first'?"

Mama sighs and puts on her coat. Luisa tries not to smile.

When they get to the World, it is dark.

Luisa holds her breath as Mama takes out her keys and opens the door.

The moment Mama turns on the light, music fills the World. Surprise!
Luisa's portraits dance along the walls and mirrors. Walter, Rupa, and
Georges have filled the room with roses and have hung tiny lights that wink
like eyes. All of Mama's favorite customers are there, dressed up, but Mama,
smiling, is the prettiest of all.

"Happy birthday!" everyone yells. Then, "Speech!"

Mama blushes. "First things first," she says, and gathers Luisa into her arms.

"For your birthday," Luisa says, "I wanted to turn the World into Roseland."

"You did, Lulu-belle," Mama says. "Thank you. . . . Thank you all."

"Mama," Luisa asks as the music swells from Walter's boom box, "will you dance with me?"

Mama doesn't move and she doesn't answer. She looks at Walter, Rupa, and Georges smiling at her. She looks at Mrs. Malloy's two old feet tapping beside her walker, like two new feet. She looks at Mrs. Fogelman's great, gray cloud of hair turned golden by the lights and changed into a clear-weather cloud. She looks at Mr. Anselmo and Hazel Mae Dixon and Mrs. Rodriguez and Mrs. Koo all dressed in their finest clothes to honor her. Then she looks deep into Luisa's eyes, and Luisa sees that Mama's eyes are no longer far away. They are near and clear and wet with tears. "Shall we dance?" Mama asks Luisa.

And Mama and Luisa dance! They twirl and whirl and laugh together.
Soon everyone is dancing, and the World seems to sparkle and spin faster
and faster around them.

Then Mr. Anselmo, with a bow so deep that his bald spot shows (and he doesn't even care!), asks Mama and Luisa to dance with him . . . and they do!

And the way Mr. Anselmo smiles at Mama and the
way she smiles back at him make Luisa think there is no
more beautiful place in the world than *this* world —

the world they are dancing in now.